Lineberger Memorial Library

Lutheran Theological Southern Seminary   Columbia, S. C.

THISTLE

BY WALTER WANGERIN, JR.

ILLUSTRATIONS BY BRYNA WALDMAN

Augsburg
MINNEAPOLIS

For my children,
whose tears I know too well,
whose laughter is as dazzling
as an answered prayer.

THISTLE

1995 Augsburg edition

Text copyright © 1995 Walter Wangerin, Jr. Illustrations copyright © 1995 Bryna Waldman.

Published in association with the literary agency of Alive Communications, P.O. Box 49068, Colorado Springs, CO 80949.

Library of Congress Catologing-in-Publication Data

Wangerin, Walter.
     Thistle / by Walter Wangerin, Jr. ; illustrations by Bryna
  Waldman.
      p.   cm.
     Summary: Of all the potato farmer's children, only gentle Thistle
can stop the terrible potato monster from destroying them.
     ISBN 0-8066-2837-5
     [1. Fairy tales.]   I. Waldman, Bryna, ill.   II. Title.
PZ8.W1965Th   1995
[E]--dc20
                                            95-9447
                                            CIP
                                            AC

Manufactured in the U.S.A.   AF 9-2837

99   98   97   96   2   3   4   5   6   7   8   9   10

Once upon a time there lived a man and a woman in a potato house. The house wasn't made of potatoes. It was called the potato house because that's what the good man did. That was his work. He grew potatoes.

All day long, every day of the summer, he went to the fields and plowed and planted. He weeded and watered potato bushes. And when the leaves turned brown, he dug in the earth—he dug to the roots where potatoes grow and pulled out bushels and bushels for people to eat.

But every day too, exactly at noon, the man went back to his house, threw open the door and hollered, "I'm hungry! Good wife, I am hungry and ready to eat. Let's have potatoes!"

It was a happy life, and they were happy people. There was only one thing that made them sad. They had no children. In the afternoons when he weeded the fields and she made soup in the kitchen, the man and the woman felt lonely for children.

So every night they folded their hands and prayed, "Dear God, do you think we could have a baby or two?"

And very soon, they did.

They had a son.

Ah, he was a tall lad! He stood like a tree, slender, straight and proud, his head thrown back, his nose on high, his eyes as green as needles. The man and the woman called him Pine, and they smiled because a family of two plus one is three.

Soon they had another son. This boy was very strong. His legs were like two trunks, his back like the bark of a mighty tree, his arms all hard with muscle. So the man and the woman called him Oak, and they laughed because three plus one is four.

Again God answered their prayer, and here came a daughter so pretty her parents got tears just looking at her. Her skin was like petals, pale and pink. The blush on her cheek was red and rare. And her neck was a tender, bending flower stalk. So they called her Rose, and they wept for gladness. Four plus one is five, and five is such a lovely number.

Then one more baby was born in the potato house. A girl. Not tall, she was short. Not strong, she was round and chubby, clumsy and soft. And plain. This child was as plain as a window weed. The man and the woman loved her very much, but because they were an honest couple they named her Thistle, and they said to God, "Six is a nice number. Six is enough."

So six is where the family stopped, and the man and the woman were lonely no longer. They were smiling. They were happy.

That is, they were happy most of the time—but not when Thistle cried. It broke their hearts when the youngest one cried. And every day, just as the man went out to work in the fields, little Thistle covered her eyes and cried.

Pine said, "Shortness, Shortness, why are you crying?"

Oak said, "She can't help it. Fatness always cries."

"Oh, Thistle!" said Rose. "Can you do nothing but cry?"

But the woman frowned at her older children and took the little one on her lap and whispered, "Thistle, what is the matter?"

Thistle said, "Papa is gone. I miss my papa."

"So that's the reason you are sad," the good woman said. "Well, wait a while and he will be home again."

And soon he was home indeed. Exactly at noon, every noon of the year, the good man stood in the doorway and hollered, "I'm hungry! Family, I'm hungry and ready to eat. Let's have potatoes!"

Now it happened one morning that, while he was digging potatoes with a sharp new shovel, the good man heard a groaning under the ground.

"Mmmmmm."

He got down on his knees and listened. "Mmmmmm." He began to dig the earth with his bare hands—and soon he felt a potato, a huge potato, a tuber bigger than any he'd ever met before.

The more he dug, the more he saw. It had rough skin and eyes all over and lumps, one lump on each side and two lumps like legs at the end of it. But this particular potato was enormous! It was twice the size of the man himself.

Suddenly one of its eyes popped open and stared straight at the man.

The man jumped backward. He had never been stared at by a potato before.

The four lumps jerked and started to move. Like arms and legs they kicked the dirt, and the giant potato climbed out of the hole and stood up! Other eyes blinked and opened. A thousand potato eyes rolled around until they were all glaring at the poor man, who was so frightened that he couldn't move.

Then the potato began to talk.

"My name is Pudge!" it roared. "And hungry!" it thundered. "I'm hungry, hungry, and ready to eat!" Oh, what a horrible roaring it made, as thick as brown gravy. "And here is my dinner before me," Pudge bellowed. "Man, I'm going to eat you!"

So that is exactly what Pudge the potato did: ate the good man, shoes, shovel and all.

Then up on bumpish legs Pudge walked to the good man's house. Exactly at noon the huge potato kicked open the door and roared, "I'm hungry!"

Inside the house was the man's whole family, his wife and all his children.

"My name is Pudge," Pudge bellowed. "I'm hungry, hungry, and ready to eat. And, Woman, I'm going to eat you!"

Which is what Pudge did—swallowed the woman completely down, then turned and stomped away.

So there stood Pine perpendicular, and Oak so muscle-bound, and Rose in a pretty faint—and Thistle. Four children all alone in the potato house, and the youngest one was crying.

"Oh, Thistle," said Pine, "can you do nothing but cry? No, nothing but cry."

Then he drew himself up straight and proud. "I," he said, "I am the oldest. I am also the tallest and the smartest. Therefore it is my job to save us. I am going out into the wide world to find some weapon for fighting the ugly Pudge, and we will be right after all."

Oak slapped his brother on the back. Rose praised him prettily. And Thistle cried. "I will miss you, Pine," she said.

Pine said, "Hush! I'll be back soon enough." And he left.

For a long, long time Pine traveled the wide world. He strode down country roads. He followed trails through the tangled woods. He looked high and low and here and there, seeking some weapon with which to fight Pudge, some magical something—but he could find nothing at all.

Then through the trees he noticed an ancient Beldame sitting on a stump. She was a hideous thing! So hunched was she that her knees reached over her ears. Her nose stuck out ten inches in front of her face, all covered with warts and dripping. Her chin stuck out ten inches too, hairy and covered with drool—and the tips of nose and chin touched like a scissors when she talked. There were exactly three grey hairs on the top of her bald head. Worst of all, she was smiling!

So ugly was the Beldame that Pine planned to pass her staring at the sky and whistling, pretending that there were no ancient Beldames anywhere in sight.

But she raised an arm as skinny as sticks, and she spoke.

"Handsome lad," she croaked, her nose and her chin snapping together, "where be thee going?"

"Madame, no business of yours," Pine said without stopping.

"Ahhh!" the Beldame cried, "I can read the green of thine eye, lad. 'Tis a weapon thou seekest! For 'twas a Pudge did gobble thy father down and thy mother too, and now thou art bound to fight a Pudge thyself."

Pine paused at such knowledge. Pine stopped altogether, looked down on oldness as bent as a toad, and said, "So?"

"So, lad—so, laddy," the Beldame cried, "I can give thee such weapons as will make a potato's tummy ache."

"Right!" said Pine, stretching forth his hand. "Give and I'll be gone, hag."

"Whisht! Not so hasty!" the Beldame screeched, grinning. "We'll make a trade of it," she said. "First let me give thee something that pleasures me, and *then* will I give thee the weapons, too."

"What can please a hag as old as you?" Pine asked.

"Why, kisses, lad!" screamed the Beldame. "Ten kisses from these wrinkled lips. 'Tis a nose and a chin have stopped my sweetest kissing, and never may I kiss again except some kind child be willing to receive it. Aye," the Beldame whispered, "but I have been so lonely so long. Green Eyes, let me kiss thee."

Well, Pine didn't even think about her trade. He drew himself up to his most splendid height, extended his long arm downward, and said, "I'll take the weapons, thank you. As for the kisses, keep them. How could I put my handsomeness between a warty nose and a slippery chin?"

The ancient Beldame fell silent. Down went her head between her knees, down, down as low as the stump. Thin went her eyes, as thin as whips. She smiled a sort of thorny smile, and softly she began to sing:

"Then take thee, Pine, what is thy due,
A clutch of weapons fit for you:
No bow nor blade nor studded boots.
No need of these—*thou shalt have roots!*"

Roots, thought Pine. Good! Anything given to one as smart as he must surely be worthy, fine weapons for fighting Pudge.

Home, then, he ran at very high speeds.

Nobly he took a stand inside the potato house. Taller and prouder than ever was he, his eyes bright green with excitement, for he was about to fight the most glorious fight of all.

He stood facing the door, waiting, waiting. His brother and sisters crouched behind him. Exactly at noon the door flew open, and there was Pudge, a thousand eyes a-blazing.

Pine threw back his head and raised his arms, ready to learn what sort of weapons *roots* might be, ready to attack.

"My name is Pudge!" the potato bellowed. "I'm hungry, hungry, and ready to eat! And, Toothpick, I'm going to eat you!"

Pine tried to jump at Pudge. But he couldn't. He tried to run, but he couldn't do that either. He was absolutely fixed to the floor. By *roots*!

So Pudge rolled forward to the poor, immobile Pine, opened a monstrous maw and swallowed the fellow down, then turned and stomped away.

Take two from six and four is left. And one from four is three. Now there were only three children left in the potato house, and one of these was crying.

"Hush, Thistle, hush!" said Oak. "Can you do nothing but cry?"

And Rose said, "No, nothing but cry."

"But I never cry," said Oak to his sisters. "And I am strong, the strongest of all," he said. "A man of few words, a man of action am I. Therefore, girls, I'm off to find the weapon Pine could not."

"Oak!" Thistle called. "Oak, I will miss you."

Too late. He was already gone, marching abroad as if he were an entire army, barking the steps as he went: "Hut, two, three, four! Hut, two, three, four!"

As it happened, Oak followed the same route Pine had taken. Soon, then, he was passing the ancient Beldame on her stump, who dripped from the tip of her nose, who drooled at her chin.

"Strong swain!" she cried. "Where be thee going so mighty and sure?"

"To war," Oak shouted, "two, three, four!"

"What!" screamed the Beldame. "Is the world at war and I knew it not?"

"Tut-tut, Elder! No need to know what doesn't concern you. I go to gain a victory. I lack but the weapons to do it."

"Weapons, weapons, the world wants weapons," muttered the Beldame, "whereas I sit here full of the cunningest weapons for cutting Pudges to bits . . ."

"Pudges?" cried Oak. He stopped and faced the skinny Beldame. "Did you say Pudges?"

"The sort of Pudges as gobble people. Aye."

"Well," said Oak, "give me your weapons and I'll leave you in peace. I'm a man of action and very few words!"

"And 'tis action I seek," yelled the Beldame. "Prithee, brave soldier, let's come to terms—a thing for a thing between us. Let me give thee what pleasures me, and then I'll give what thou needest."

"Whatever," Oak said.

"Ahhh!" shrieked the ancient Beldame. "He saith *whatever*! A generous answer, that."

"Terms, Elder! Tell me your terms and I'll go."

Slowly and sweetly she whispered, "To kiss thee."

"What?"

"Aye, I long to be less lonely. To find one soldier brave enough to brush these withered lips. To give thee, sir, five kisses only, after which I'll give thee such wonderful weapons . . ."

Oak made a fist and pounded his chest. "I am a fighter, not a lover!" he shouted. "Forget about kisses. Give me weapons!"

Once again the Beldame's head sank down until her two knees touched above it. Her eyes grew sharper than knives. Her cheeks went white. She smiled a freezing smile and began to sing this little song:

"Snakes and serpents, adders, newts—
For all thy muscles, substitutes!
I'll send thee, soldier,
Home the bolder:
Strong, strong Oak, *Thou shalt have roots!*"

"HUT-TWO-THREE-FOUR! HUTTWOTHREEFOUR . . ."

Right away, Oak was galloping back to the potato house, counting the steps and whooping as he went. "Roots? Roots? Whatever!" he cried. "Soldiers can fight with any weapon!"

He pushed his sisters out of the way and stood foursquare before the door.

BOOM! The door flew open. The monstrous potato was here.

"My name is Pudge!" Pudge bellowed. "I'm hungry, hungry, and ready to eat! And, Acorn, I'm going to eat you!"

If Oak was strong, then roots were stronger. They held the poor boy so fast to the floor that he could neither run nor fight. Instead, he was swallowed, and the great Pudge turned and stomped away.

ne from three leaves two. Two sisters alone were left in the potato house, and one of these was crying.

"Oh, Thistle," Rose scolded, "can you do nothing but cry? No, nothing but cry. I, on the other hand, have a plan. Thistle," she said, "do you see how beautiful I am?"

Thistle nodded. No one could help but see how beautiful Rose was.

"Well, beauty is better than muscles or brains because beauty can turn the foe against himself! Wait here," said Rose. "I'll be back in a bit."

"Rose, I will miss you," poor Thistle cried.

But Rose was already gone. Skipping lightly, humming a silly tune, she was traveling through the world, and soon, just like her brothers before her, she saw the ancient Beldame crouched on a stump.

For just a moment she was shocked to find so much ugliness in one spare body.

But then she took control of herself and stared straight ahead with icy eyes, waiting for the Beldame to notice the difference between the two of them and be properly ashamed.

The Beldame, however, knew no shame. Neither did she spend time chatting with this particular child. Bluntly she croaked the terms of her trade: "Weapons for kisses, my pretty," she said. "Let me give thee but a single kiss, and then I shall dress thee in wonderful weapons."

Rose was not surprised by the request. The stones themselves would kiss her if they had lips and she gave them permission.

But she tossed her head and said, "Those who someday kiss me will be worthy of the favor. That's one or two, just one or two in all the world. And you," Rose sniffed, "are not among them."

The ancient Beldame nodded and nodded as if this were a pretty saying, suitable for remembering. But so low did her old head go this time, that her chin was scratching the ground. So slitty were her eyes that they could have cut. And so softly did the Beldame sing, that Rose could scarcely hear the song:

> "The Rose that loves the rosebud best
> Deserves what I gave all the rest;
> Dost love thy form? Thy stem? Thy shoots?
> Take one thing more: *Thou shalt have roots.*

Rose neither blinked nor blanched. She shrugged and said, "My brothers never knew what to do with your gift. Roots, is it? Well, I will take your evil and make it my good."

The ancient Beldame closed her eyes with a smile as bleak as winter.

But Rose tripped lightly home again, told Thistle to keep to her place, then turned to wait for Pudge.

Exactly at noon the door flew open, and there was Pudge gazing with a thousand eyes at the lovely and limpid Rose.

"Sugar!" Pudge bellowed. "I'm hungry, hungry, and ready to eat . . . some sugar!"

Rose showed no fear. Instead, she smiled and said, "Come to me, dear. I am sweetness indeed."

As Pudge approached, then, she raised her hands—and with the long soft roots that grew from her fingers, she began to caress the potato. She tossed thin roots over the shoulders and down the back; she ran ropes of roots around the stubby arms.

She had just begun to tangle Pudge in a net of tender knots when Thistle, seeing the monster so close to her sister, screamed: "Rosy, Rosy, what are you doing?"

Rose turned and shouted, "Shut up!"

And in that instant, Pudge shook free. He roared, "DESSERT!" and swallowed the beautiful Rose all in a single gulp.

Six were four, and four but two, and two no more than one.

Poor Thistle, the youngest of them all, was left alone in the potato house, crying.

"Thistle, Thistle," she said to herself, "can you do nothing but cry? No, nothing but cry," she said.

The tears fell down like rain. Her sighs were like wind in the house.

"Oh, I wish I were tall," she said. But she was short.

"I wish I were strong." But she was weak.

"And how I wish I were beautiful." But she was as plain as a window weed, nothing of value, nothing to use in the fight against Pudge, nothing, no, nothing but tears.

Thistle stumbled from the house. She wandered into the world with neither a thought nor a plan. She had nowhere to go. All the world was lonely now. Potato fields were flat and empty. The sky was cold and grey. And Thistle was missing everybody.

She walked and walked, crying out loud and naming the names of her family: "Pine, I miss you!" she sobbed. "Oak, my big brother! Rosy, Rosy, pretty Rose."

Just then she heard a horrible croaking, like a warty toad speaking. "I am acquainted with those," it said. "Rose and Oak and Pine . . ."

Thistle rubbed the tears from her eyes and looked, and there on a stump was an ancient bunch-backed Beldame, as old as stone and ugly.

"Really?" the child whispered. "Did you know them too?"

"Very well indeed," the Beldame croaked.

Thistle went right over to her and put her chubby hand on the old woman's foot. "Oh, thank you," she cried. "They were my family, my brothers and sister."

"Aye," the Beldame hissed with narrow eyes, "I met them each by each, and each by each I sent them home again."

"Oh, Mother!" Thistle burst into fresh tears. "But they aren't home any more! Pudge has eaten all the height and strength and beauty in the world. What is left? What is left?"

"Little and nothing," quoth the Beldame, switching ten inches of chin in the air, "except that I may give thee something worthless to thee, but it pleasures me to give it."

Thistle sobbed, "Well, someone should have pleasure in this sad world."

The Beldame opened her eyes and stared at the child. "What?" she said. "Thou wilt take my worthless thing?"

"Yes."

"Aiee!" cried the Beldame. "And dost not ask first what I mean to give thee?"

Thistle shook her head. "You knew my sister and my dear brothers. You comfort me, Mother. I will comfort you."

"Child," breathed the ancient Beldame, "let me kiss thee."

Thistle nodded, sobbing, still sobbing. "Kiss me."

So then the Beldame slid down from her trunk and reached out crooked arms toward Thistle and kissed her. Not one kiss. Not five or ten: she kissed the child a thousand times. Every tear that Thistle shed, the Beldame kissed it.

And every tear, when it was kissed, turned into a thorn.

Soon Thistle was covered by tiny thorns, stem and leaf, hair and blossom, cheek and knee and all ten toes. And the ancient Beldame smiled a very glad smile and whispered, "Done."

Then she sang a little song:

> "Cap-a-pie and foot to brow,
> One child is weaponed now."

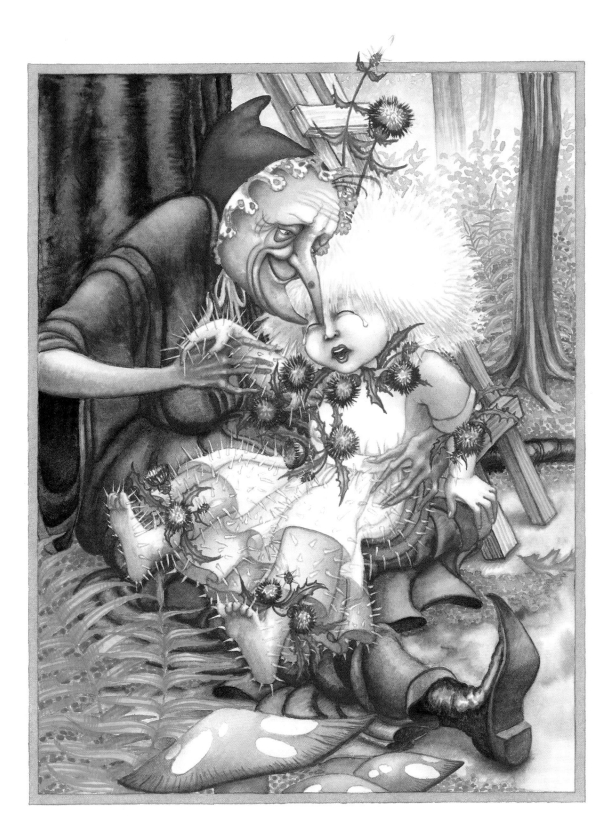

She turned back to her stump. And then, just before she entered it and disappeared, she sighed and said, "Wee Thistle, thou hast blown the chill from mine old and hoary heart. As for you, lass, go home again. Wait thee there for Pudge, and we shall see what we shall see."

Thistle. Dear Thistle, with nothing else before her, did go home again.

In the very same place where Pine stood tall and Oak made muscles and Rose tried to charm the monster, Thistle came and waited, facing the door of the potato house, thinking nothing.

BOOM! Exactly at noon the door flew open.

"MY NAME IS PUDGE!" Pudge thundered into the house.

Thistle nodded. "I know," she said.

"I'M HUNGRY! HUNGRY! AND READY TO EAT!"

"Yes," said Thistle. "I thought so."

"AND, PORRIDGE," Pudge roared louder than ever before, "I'M GOING TO EAT YOU!"

"Yes," said Thistle. "Yes."

The bloated potato began to thump forward on stubby legs. Thistle sighed and bowed her head. A thousand eyes rolled all around her. An enormous mouth gaped wide above her. And then she was swallowed into the gullet of the huge potato.

But this time Pudge did not turn and stomp away.

Instead, the potato's eyes started to blink and to shed tears.

"Mmmmmm!" The potato's thick arms began to beat on the stomach, and Pudge was groaning in terrible pain:

"Mmmmmm! Mmmmmmmm-ahhh!"

For the thorns of Thistle were stinging Pudge on the inside, in all the tender places.

"WHAT DID I EAT?" Pudge bellowed, falling down to the floor. "AND WHAT IS EATING ME?"

The burning of a thousand thorns grew hotter and hotter inside the potato, huger and huger—till Pudge the potato burst at the middle, exploding all over the house.

And out of the hole came the good man, Thistle's papa, sticky with mashed potatoes, but healthy and grinning. And out came the good woman, too!

Next, Pine jumped out, a little bit bent. And Oak, somewhat weak and woozy. But both were alive and smiling.

Rose appeared, smiling too, though the bloom had gone out of her cheek a bit. Soon everyone was looking at the hole in Pudge. A father, a mother, two brothers and a sister were holding their breath and waiting, waiting . . .

Then out crept Thistle, and the whole family shouted and started to laugh!

"Thistle! Thistle!" they sang, as if her name were a song. They formed a ring and danced around her.

Yes, she was still short and chubby and plain; but all of her thorns had turned into dimples. And dimples are lovely, dimples are things that people love to touch. So her sister and brothers and mother and father touched and hugged her very much.

"Oh, Thistle! You could do nothing but cry—but tears were the best weapons after all!"

So then six were six, together again. And all who lived in the potato house were happy indeed.

And Pudge? Well, of Pudge they made potato soup.